GRANNY LEARNS TO FLY is Tony Hickey's twenty-first book for young people. Like his first, *The Matchless Mice,* it is published by The Children's Press, of which he was the co-founder.

Tony has worked extensively in radio and television. His TV dramatisations of *An Taoille Tuille* by Mairtin Ó Cadhain, and *The Ante-room* and *The Last of Summer,* both by Kate O'Brien, have sold world-wide.

His *Flip 'n' Flop* series is currently enjoying huge success, and a musical version of *The Castle of Dreams,* in collaboration with the American composer Edie Doughty, recently had its world premiere, to great acclaim, in Barbados. Further performances are planned and there is interest in the project in the USA. A recording of the piece is also under consideration.

In a recent poll of children's favourite authors, he shared third place with Enid Blyton, one of his own favourites as a child.

Tony Hickey

Granny Learns to FLY

THE CHILDREN'S PRESS

First published 1996 by
The Children's Press
an imprint of Anvil Books
45 Palmerston Road, Dublin 6

4 6 5

ISBN 0 947962 96 4

Typesetting by Computertype Limited
Printed by Colour Books Limited

Contents

1

Granny Green

Sean and Maura, the O'Brien twins, had one of the nicest grannies in the world. She was always happy and smiling, always pleased to see them and she seemed to know exactly the right presents to give them at Christmas and on their birthday. She even seemed to know when they could use a little extra pocket money, even though the twins' parents said that they must not take money from her.

Granny Green, for that was her name, just pooh-poohed that idea and would say, in the nicest way possible, 'It is my money so, please, tell your mum and dad that I will spend it any way I want to!'

The house that Granny Green lived in

was just as nice as she was. It was called 'Tigín' which, in the Irish language, means 'little house'. It stood on the edge of the Valley of the Crows in County Wicklow.

In many ways, the Valley of the Crows was like a secret, hidden valley. To get to it, you had to leave the main road and drive along several other roads that became narrower and narrower, with many twists and turns.

Most people, out for a day in the country, soon turned back, saying, 'These roads don't go anywhere at all!'

This suited Granny Green. The last thing in the world that she wanted was what she called 'day-trippers from the city' spoiling her valley with their radios and barking dogs and rubbish and smelly car fumes.

Granny Green felt somehow that she was in charge of the valley and that her little house was like a sentry-post guarding the only way into or out of it.

Once, several families had lived in the valley. Now they had all moved away, mainly to the town of Dara where the twins' parents owned a hotel. Their houses and cottages remained empty, used only occasionally in the summer for holidays, or by farmers rounding up the sheep that grazed peacefully on the thick, sweet grass that grew in the valley.

Granny Green often came into the town of Dara in her little red car to shop. Spit, her beautiful black cat, always travelled with her. He draped himself around her neck like a fur collar.

Other motorists often had a fright when the fur collar unwound itself and looked at them through the side window. This always made Granny Green chuckle.

'You bad cat!' she would say to Spit. 'You do that on purpose, just to alarm people!'

Spit would give a little miaow by way of reply and settle down once more around her shoulders.

He was called Spit because when Granny found him, one cold winter morning on the side of the road, he had hissed and spat at her when she lifted him up to take him home. He had soon settled down in Tigín and was as happy as any cat could wish to be.

2

The Little Red Car

One day Granny Green arrived in town as usual with Spit, in her little red car, and parked it outside the hotel. Then leaving Spit with her daughter, Mrs O'Brien, she went off to shop, not just for herself but also for several of her friends whose houses she passed on her way into town.

By the time she got back to her car, she was loaded down with packages and parcels. Luckily, Sean and Maura arrived home from school at the same time and were able to help her to load up the car. But when Granny Green tried to start the car, nothing happened.

Mr O'Brien came out of the hotel and looked at the engine. He could see nothing wrong with it, so he sent for Mr

Ryan, who owned the local garage, and he examined the engine of the car very carefully.

Then he shook his head. 'I'm afraid that it's a question of age.'

'Age?' Granny Green asked.

'Yes, Mrs Green, age,' explained Mr Ryan. 'Sooner or later, everything begins to wear out. That's what has happened to your car. It's worn out.'

'Can't it be fixed?' asked Mrs O'Brien.

'Oh, I dare say it could, but it would

cost several hundred pounds. And I couldn't guarantee how long it would be before it needed to be repaired again. As it is, I would have to order parts specially from Dublin. That could take, maybe, two weeks.

'I think Mrs Green should consider herself very lucky that the car didn't give up while she was driving along one of those lonely roads. She could have been stuck there for hours.'

'But I'm stuck here in Dara now,' said

Granny Green. 'Even if I had several hundred pounds – which I don't – to have the car repaired, how are Spit and I going to get back home?

'And what about my friends who are waiting for their shopping? They depend on me and my little red car. They have no other way of getting things from the town, now that there is no longer a bus service. What on earth are we all going to do?'

'I can drive you home now,' said Mrs O'Brien. 'We can stop at your friends' houses on the way and give them their shopping. You'll simply have to leave your car here outside the hotel until we decide what is the best thing to do. No good will come from worrying, Mother.'

As Granny Green and Spit and all the shopping were driven off by Mrs O'Brien, the twins and Mr O'Brien felt very sad about what had happened. Mr

O'Brien said, 'Next weekend, when your summer holidays begin, you will both have to cycle out to Tigín and make sure that your granny is all right. This couldn't have happened at a worse time. Your mum and I are up to our eyes with work. The hotel has never been so busy.'

'If only Granny was on the telephone, we could call her and try to cheer her up,' said Sean.

'Well, since she isn't on the phone,' sighed Mr O'Brien, 'what can't be cured must be endured.'

3

A Mystery

On the following Saturday morning, as soon as breakfast was over, Maura and Sean set off on their bicycles for Tigín.

It was a perfect day for cycling. The sun was not too hot. A light breeze danced over the countryside. The hedges were in full bloom. The leaves on the trees were green and fresh. Ditches were filled with primroses. The curve of the river was bright with wild irises. Birds were singing.

Some of Granny Green's friends were out working in their gardens. They waved and smiled as the twins whizzed past.

'They don't seem very worried,' said Sean.

'Maybe they've found an answer to

the problem of how to manage without Granny's car,' replied Maura.

They whizzed around the last bend in the road and reached Granny Green's house. She was very surprised to see them. 'I didn't expect you today,' she said.

'We came to see if you're all right,' said Maura.

'Oh, I'm fine,' Granny Green said. 'Just fine.'

But, unlike her friends in their gardens, she didn't behave as though she was fine. Instead, she moved nervously around her sitting-room. She patted cushions that did not need to be patted. She straightened tablecloths that did not need to be straightened. She touched her hair as though she thought it was not properly in place.

Spit was not his usual self either. He refused to let the twins pet him and jumped up on the dresser, well out of their reach.

For the first time ever, the twins felt unwelcome in Granny Green's house. By just being there, they seemed to be making Granny and Spit uneasy.

'Maybe we should think of getting back for our lunch,' Sean said.

'Oh yes,' Granny Green said eagerly. 'You don't want to be late for your lunch, especially on a Saturday.'

Ordinarily Granny Green would have insisted that the twins stay and have lunch with her. She might even have insisted that they spend the weekend with her. They kept spare clothes in her house for when that happened. But now, Granny Green – and, in his own way, Spit the cat – was hardly able to hide her eagerness to see the twins leave.

As the twins headed back to the town, Maura said, 'I feel there is something seriously wrong.'

'I know,' said Sean, 'but what could it be that is making both her and Spit so jumpy? I don't think it has to do with the car. She'd have told us if that was what was worrying her.'

'You don't suppose it's something terrible like blackmail, do you?' asked Maura, and then she was so shocked at that idea that she lost control of her bicycle. It crashed into Sean's. They both ended up in the ditch.

Sean, as shocked as Maura at the idea of Granny Green being blackmailed, didn't even complain at being knocked into the ditch. Instead he just lay there and considered the idea.

Then he said, 'But what could anyone blackmail Granny Green about? She is one of the nicest, kindest, happiest people in the world ... or at least she was until this morning.'

'Which only goes to prove how serious the situation must be,' said Maura.

'I think we should try and find out what's going on.'

Before they could move, they heard a car coming along the road. They popped their heads up out of the ditch in time to catch a glimpse of it before it vanished

from sight around the next bend.

'That looked very like Mrs Fitzgerald's car,' said Sean.

Mrs Fitzgerald lived in the middle of the town and was the same age as Granny Green as well as being one of her closest friends.

'I've never known her to drive as fast as that before,' said Maura. 'In fact, she usually refuses to drive at all if she can help it.'

Sean said, 'Maybe Granny was expecting Mrs Fitzgerald to call and didn't want us to be there when she arrived. Maybe that was why she was so nervous!'

'But why should she mind the two of us being in the house at the same time as Mrs Fitzgerald? Unless ...' and here Maura's eyes became as large as saucers, 'unless it is Mrs Fitzgerald who is doing the blackmailing!'

Mrs Fitzgerald a blackmailer? Nice, fluffy Mrs Fitzgerald with her pink frocks and blue hair?

'Never!' said Sean. 'Mrs Fitzgerald would never blackmail anyone even if she knew the most terrible things about them. Unless, of course, she's being blackmailed as well and has rushed out to Granny Green with details of the latest demand.'

'We're wasting time talking,' said Maura. 'Let's leave the bikes in the ditch. We'll go back to Granny Green's on foot and see what we can discover. We can come back for the bikes later.'

The twins hurried back down the road. They kept well within the shadows of the trees, knowing that this would make it difficult for them to be seen.

Mrs Fitzgerald's car was parked outside Granny Green's gate. The front door of the little house opened. Mrs Fitzgerald and Granny Green came out. Granny was carrying a large cardboard box. The two women glanced around as if to make sure that they were not being watched. Then they got into the car and drove into the valley.

The twins looked at each other. What on earth could be in that box?

'The door is open,' Maura said.

'What?'

'The front door of the cottage is open. Granny didn't close it properly.'

'Which just goes to show how very worried she and Mrs Fitzgerald must be,' said Sean. 'Still, it's our chance to have a quick look around inside for clues.'

24

But there were no clues to be found in the cottage. It looked the way it always did, except that not only was Granny gone; so too was Spit!

'Spit must have been in that box that Granny was carrying,' said Maura. 'But why is she taking him into the valley in Mrs Fitzgerald's car? The only time I've ever seen Spit in a box was when he was sick and had to be taken to the vet.'

'He was acting a bit strange this morning,' Sean pointed out.

'Yes, but he wasn't sick. And anyway, the vet is in Dara, not in the valley.'

Before Sean could even consider what Maura had said, they heard another car being driven past Tigín. They rushed to the window but were able to catch just the briefest glimpse of it before it sped into the valley.

'We didn't even get the licence number,' said Sean. 'It could well have been the blackmailer going to meet Granny and Mrs Fitzgerald.

'Hey, maybe Granny brought Spit with her in case there was an attempt to steal him while she was out of the house. That happens all the time on TV. People are tricked into leaving their house, and while they are out something precious is stolen!'

'Except that this isn't TV,' said Maura. 'Anyway, blackmailers usually want money, not cats. Unless Granny is being forced to give Spit as a hostage!'

'Granny would never do that, no matter what was likely to happen to her,' said Sean.

Then he noticed a pair of goggles on the window ledge. They were exactly like the goggles motor-cyclists used to wear long ago.

'Where did these come from?' He held them up for Maura to see. 'And why

would Granny need them?'

'The answers to all our questions must be in the valley,' said Maura. 'The best thing for us to do is to go on into the valley and try to find out more about what's going on there. Then we can go back to Dara and tell Mum and Dad.'

'OK,' said Sean. 'But we will have to be very careful not to be seen. That means going across the fields.'

4

A Council of War

The sun was hotter as the twins left Tigín and started their journey along the valley. The only sound was the chatter of a stream tumbling towards the river. The only visible living creatures were small groups of sheep, watching as the twins dodged from one clump of gorse to another and then to the shelter of one of the many huge rocks that were dotted around the fields.

They were almost half way along the valley when Sean grabbed Maura's arm and pointed to a clump of tall, dark trees. 'What's in there?' he asked.

'It's the old Durcan farmhouse,' said Maura. 'It's been empty for years.'

'I wasn't referring to the house,' said Sean. 'I was pointing at the cars parked near it. What are they doing there?'

Maura narrowed her eyes against the glare of the sun and looked more carefully towards the farmhouse and the trees. Sean was right! There were at least four cars parked among the trees.

Anyone going along the road would have found the cars very difficult to see. To the twins, looking down from behind a huge rock, they were just about visible.

'I'll bet Mrs Fitzgerald's car is one of them,' said Sean.

And that was all he had time to say before there was a loud WHOOSH and something passed right above their heads. Terrified, he and Maura fell flat on the ground.

'What was that?' Maura whispered.

'I don't know,' Sean whispered back.

Then they heard the same sound as before, WHOOSH, coming back over their heads! This time they forced themselves to look up. Their mouths fell open!

There, high in the sky, was nice, fluffy little Mrs Fitzgerald, moving through the air as easily as if she were floating in a swimming pool!

As she reached the top of the trees around the farmhouse, she looped the loop, rolled over and then descended, feet first, out of sight beyond the parked cars!

The twins gulped in amazement.

A dozen questions formed in their

minds, questions that remained unasked as two shadows fell over them.

They turned their heads and found themselves looking up at Mr Grogan and Miss Lynch, two of the oldest inhabitants of Dara.

'So you've come to spy on us, have you?' snapped Mr Grogan. 'Well, you may get to your feet and quick-march to the farmhouse where we will decide what's to be done with you!'

Miss Lynch glared angrily through her steel-rimmed glasses. 'Do as you are told or your granny could be in worse trouble than she is already!'

The twins realised that it was useless to protest. They allowed themselves to be led like two prisoners down to the road and in among the trees to the parked cars.

Granny Green was horrified when she saw them. She said, 'I thought you had gone back to the hotel!'

'We were going back,' said Maura. 'But we knew something was wrong, that you were very upset about something. Then we saw you getting into Mrs Fitzgerald's car...'

'And so you decided to see what you could find out,' interrupted Mr Grogan. 'I knew, as soon as your granny turned up today without her goggles and with that cat of hers, that she was far too absent-minded to be trusted.'

'That's not fair,' said Granny Green. 'You know as well as I do that where I go, Spit goes. And you are also forgetting that if it wasn't for me, none of you would be here!'

'That's right,' sneered Miss Lynch. 'Tell your grandchildren everything! Or maybe they already know more than they should!'

'We thought Granny Green was being blackmailed,' said Sean. 'That's why we came into the valley. We never expected to see Mrs Fitzgerald flying, not even when we found Granny's goggles on the window ledge. We thought they were the kind used on motorbikes!'

'And by air pilots long ago,' said Mrs Fitzgerald. 'They kept the wind out of their eyes.'

'A pity they couldn't also keep busybodies out of this valley,' said Mr

Grogan. 'These children can't go back to the hotel now. They might blab and spoil everything! '

There was a murmur of agreement from the direction of the farmhouse. Standing there, out of the glare of the sun, were several elderly people from the town. Draped across a window ledge behind them was Spit. He looked as though he had lived there all his life.

'It will make things much worse if we go missing,' said Maura. 'Mum and Dad know we came out to see Granny. If we don't show up at the hotel, search parties will be out looking for us.'

'The children are right,' said Mrs Fitzgerald. 'Maybe if they were to give us their solemn promise not to say a word about what they have seen here...'

'We can't afford to rely on a promise,' said Miss Lynch. 'Supposing they forget and let something slip!'

'Supposing they stayed with their granny until "the big day"?' said Mrs Fitzgerald.

'But that's a week away,' said Granny Green. 'Their parents would suspect that there was something wrong if they stayed that long. Could the big day not be sooner?'

'It could have been today if it wasn't for you,' said Miss Lynch.

'I know,' said Granny Green sadly. 'But I just can't help feeling nervous.'

'All you have to do is follow the instructions in the book,' said Mrs Fitzgerald. '*I* managed without any difficulty.'

'It's that cat of hers, that's the real problem!' Mr Grogan glared at Spit as he spoke.

Spit glared right back at him and swished his tail as though saying, 'Who do you think *you're* talking about?'

'It just wouldn't be fair for me to go flying without Spit,' said Granny. 'After all, he always travels with me in the car!'

'I think Spit would behave no matter where you took him,' said Maura. 'I bet he'd love to go flying.'

As if to prove that this was true, Spit jumped down off the window ledge and strolled over to Granny Green.

'Oh, the dote!' said Granny Green. 'I sometimes think he understands every word I say.'

Spit went 'Miaow!' as though objecting to the word 'sometimes'.

'I'll do it,' Granny decided. 'I'll try and fly right now.'

5

Granny has a Go!

Mr Grogan signalled to everyone to be silent.

Granny Green closed her eyes and seemed to go into a trance. Several minutes passed. Then Granny opened her eyes, picked Spit up and draped him around her shoulders.

She then took a few steps backwards and ran forward.

She hovered a few centimetres above the ground, but then her feet came back to earth.

She tried again. This time, she hovered several metres above the ground before touching down again.

For the third attempt she closed her eyes and took a much longer run before leaving the ground. She went higher

than before into the air!

Then suddenly she took off and soared above the trees just as Mrs Fitzgerald had done.

She flew over the farmhouse and over the parked cars and landed, shakily but safely, next to the twins.

'You did it! You did it!' Sean and Maura shouted.

'A bit more practice and you will be perfect,' said Mrs Fitzgerald. 'And just look at Spit! He couldn't be happier.'

And indeed Spit was positively smiling as he jumped down from Granny's shoulders and purred around her feet.

'Well, we could have the big day on Monday,' said Mr Grogan. 'It's early closing day for most of the shops in Dara. But what about the twins?'

'They could spend the weekend with me without causing any problems,' said Granny. 'If someone would just call into the hotel and tell their parents.'

'I'll do that,' said Miss Lynch. 'Now on with the practice!'

For the next half-hour, all the elderly people took turns at flying. Some of them were very good. Others, like Granny Green, were a bit shaky to start with but soon improved.

'Right,' smiled Mr Grogan. 'That's enough for today. Please get into the car in which you drove here. And don't everyone drive off at once.'

'That's so no one will notice and wonder why there were so many cars in the valley at the same time,' explained Granny as she and the twins, with Spit in his box, settled into Mrs Fitzgerald's car.

'It won't mean too many nasty fumes around the place either,' said Sean. 'But please, *please* tell us just what's been happening.'

'I suppose no harm will come from telling you the full story now,' said Granny Green. 'In a way, it all started last Tuesday when the car broke down. After your mother dropped me off at my place, I suddenly realised just how helpless I would be without a car. And there were lots of other people of my age with cars who no longer feel comfortable driving.'

'Like me,' said Mrs Fitzgerald. 'My eyesight is not as good as it used to be.'

For a moment, the twins wondered if that was why she was driving so fast. Maybe she couldn't read the speedometer. But they said nothing as Mrs Fitzgerald continued, 'That's why I don't drive nearly as much as I used to.'

'And Mr Grogan's insurance company want him to have a medical exam next year to see if he's still fit to drive,' said Granny Green. 'As for poor Miss Lynch, her arthritis is getting worse and

41

worse. Yet she finds she can fly without any problem at all, just as Mrs Fitzgerald can, even without her glasses!'

'There's something about being up in the sky that makes me see so clearly,' said Mrs Fitzgerald.

'But you still haven't told us *how* you came to be able to fly,' said Maura.

'Oh well, as I was saying, after your mother dropped me off at Tigín last Tuesday, I felt very worried and very sad at the thought of not having a car to get around in,' said Granny Green. 'But I knew that the worst thing for a person to do is to sit around feeling sorry for herself, so I decided that I must find something useful to do. And I knew what that thing should be: to tidy the attic.'

The twins had never been allowed into the attic above their granny's bedroom. As far as they knew, their mother hadn't been either. It was considered far too dirty and dusty. Indeed, Granny herself hadn't been up there since she was a child. But on the afternoon that her little red car broke down, she had tied an old scarf around her head, put on old clothes, fetched the step-ladder from the shed and opened the trapdoor into the attic.

6

The Secret in the Attic

The attic was in a worse state than she had expected. Years and years of cobwebs hung everywhere like thick lace curtains. Spit, who had followed Granny, left pawprints in the dust, which looked like grey snow.

Granny Green had almost changed her mind about tidying the place. She couldn't decide where to begin.

Then Spit had rushed forward after a huge spider that scuttled for shelter in a corner. He knocked against a pile of books and picture frames. These crashed to the ground with such a clatter and raised such a cloud of dust that Spit and Granny thought the roof was coming in. They also began to sneeze because of the dust.

Terrified, Spit ran towards the trap-door.

'It's all right,' Granny had said to Spit. 'You haven't done any real harm …'

Then she saw an old black trunk that had belonged to her great-grandmother and which no one, as far as she could remember, had ever opened because the key had been misplaced.

Granny's own mother had said, 'The key must be somewhere in the house. It would be a shame to break the lock when we might yet find the key.'

Now there was no need for a key. The lock was so old that it fell off when Granny touched it. Inside the trunk, carefully wrapped in a piece of cloth, was a huge book with the name of Granny Green's great-grandmother written in it.

Inside the book, written in the same handwriting, were all kinds of advice and recipes, almost like spells. The last chapter was called 'How to Fly'.

Granny Green forgot all about cleaning the attic. Instead she carried the book down into her sitting-room where she spent the rest of the evening reading it. She was especially interested in the last chapter.

'It just occurred to me that all our problems would be solved if we could fly,' explained Granny Green as Mrs Fitzgerald drove them out of the valley.

'And it seemed so easy. You just had to think yourself into the right frame of mind and convince yourself that you could do it.'

'Like athletes do before they run a race,' said Maura.

'I never thought of it like that but, yes, I suppose you're right,' Granny Green smiled. 'Anyway, just as I finished reading the chapter, who should call to the front door but Mr Grogan. I'd been in his shop earlier on to buy a book that I was looking forward to reading. I left it behind on the counter and he was kind enough to bring it out to me.'

'So you told him about your great-grandmother's book,' said Sean.

'I not only told him but I made him read the chapter on "How to Fly",' replied Granny Green. 'Of course, being Mr Grogan, he wouldn't believe a word of it, said it was all nonsense. But I persuaded him that we ought at least to try it, in case it worked. So we agreed that he would ask people that we knew we could trust to meet us at the old Durcan farmhouse the next day, just to see what would happen. And it *did* work!

'Once people began to see how flying could solve their problems, they managed to get themselves into the right frame of mind and actually start to fly.'

'So now it doesn't matter whether or not your little red car gets fixed,' said Maura.

'Exactly,' said Granny Green. 'And no more pollution from petrol fumes!'

'It's the most wonderful thing I've ever heard,' said Sean. 'But what did you mean when you talked about "the big day"?'

'Oh, that's the day when we will show the people of Dara what we can do,' said Mrs Fitzgerald. 'If we'd said anything sooner, someone would be bound to say that flying was too dangerous for elderly people.'

'That's one of the problems of getting old,' said Granny Green. 'People begin to treat you as though you are helpless, and yet they don't do very much to give you a helping hand. Still, we'll show them on Monday afternoon!'

'Do you think we could learn to fly too?' asked Maura.

'I have a feeling that maybe it's something that only elderly people can

49

do,' said Granny Green. 'Or people who really *need* to be able to fly. Now I'm sure we could all do with a nice glass of lemonade while I get lunch ready. Mrs Fitzgerald, you'll stay and eat with us, won't you?'

'I'd be delighted,' said Mrs Fitzgerald, stopping her car so suddenly outside the gate of Tigín that Granny, the twins and Spit fell into a heap.

As they clambered out of the car, Maura asked, 'Why did you put Spit in the cardboard box?'

'Oh, because he wasn't used to Mrs Fitzgerald's car,' replied Granny Green. 'I wasn't sure how he would behave. But I had no need to worry, did I, Spit?'

The twins could have sworn that Spit said, 'Of course not,' but then decided that they were imagining things.

All next day, the twins acted as look-outs while the elderly people practised flying. Fortunately no one else came near the valley and, by evening, everyone felt confident that they were as good at flying as they would ever be.

'Right then,' said Mr Grogan. 'Time for the posters and a telephone call to the local radio station. I hope you will all listen in tomorrow?'

'Oh, indeed we will, indeed we will,' everyone replied.

7

A Flying Display

Next morning, Monday, at the start of the big day, Granny Green tuned into the local radio station.

She and the twins were just in time to hear the announcer say, 'Well, strange things seem to be happening in the little town of Dara. People woke this morning to find posters all over the place advertising a flying display in the Valley of the Crows, just seven miles outside the town. The question that everyone is asking is: who exactly is giving this flying display and, indeed, will they be allowed to give it?

'We had a quick word with the Minister of Defence first thing this morning – sorry, Minister, if we interrupted your beauty sleep – and he says that he

knows nothing about any flying display. Furthermore, he says that any such display would be against the law and that he will do all in his power to prevent it happening.'

Granny Green roared with laughter. 'He must be expecting jet planes and helicopters and all kinds of things to go flying around the place.'

'Instead of which it will be Granny Green and Co!' said Sean.

'And her famous cat,' added Maura.

By three o'clock in the afternoon, the road to the valley was jammed with cars and vans and motorcycles. A police car blocked the entrance to the valley to prevent anyone driving in there. Loudspeakers told the people, who had left their vehicles and walked the last mile or so, to go home.

'There will be no flying display here this afternoon,' the voice kept saying. 'You are wasting your time. Kindly turn around and go home!'

But, even if anyone felt like heeding this advice, the crowd was now too big for people to be able to turn back. The twins pointed to the high ground close to the farmhouse. 'You'll see better from there,' they said.

People were so excited that they did as the twins suggested. No one even asked them what they knew about this flying display. Then they found themselves talking to their parents.

'Don't tell me that the two of you are mixed up in all this,' said Mr O'Brien.

'It will be all right, honestly it will,' the twins said.

Suddenly there was the sound of loud music from the farmhouse. Granny and Co had fixed up their own loudspeaker system, which filled the valley with waltz music.

The crowd, including Mr and Mrs O'Brien, became very quiet. Then, in time to the music, Granny Green, with Spit draped around her shoulders, flew up over the clump of trees.

Then came Mrs Fitzgerald and Mr Grogan and Miss Lynch. Then came the rest of the elderly people.

The watching crowd gasped and applauded and cried out in amazement as Granny and Co swooped and circled and turned, always in time to the music.

Then as the music came to an end, the flyers gracefully descended out of sight behind the trees.

The crowd went wild. None of them had ever imagined, much less seen, anything like the flying display. Dozens of people surged forward towards the farmhouse.

Granny Green's voice came over the loudspeakers. 'Please do not trample on the grass any more than is necessary or frighten the sheep. Please go back to Dara. We will come and explain everything to you as soon as you have taken all your cars and vans and motorcycles home.'

The crowd was so impressed by the firmness of Granny's voice and so anxious to hear the full story that immediately people began to leave the valley. Soon only Mr and Mrs O'Brien and the twins remained.

Granny Green came out from among the trees and hurried towards them. 'I'm sorry I couldn't let you into the secret sooner,' she said to Mr and Mrs O'Brien. 'But, if you'll give us a lift back to Dara, the twins and I will explain everything.'

When Granny explained, Mr and Mrs O'Brien were amazed! So too were the people gathered around the hotel. Television crews had by now turned up with their cameras. So had reporters from the national newspapers and radio stations.

Within hours, there were special editions of the evening papers on the city streets with headlines like: GRANNY GREEN TAKES TO THE SKIES!, A NEW AGE DAWNS FOR OUR SENIOR CITIZENS!, SPIT GETS A BIRD'S-EYE VIEW OF THE WORLD!

Granny Green and her friends were now the most famous people not just in Ireland but in the whole world. There was serious talk of setting up flying schools for the elderly wherever they were needed.

'I just hope that it will work as well for people elsewhere as it did for us in the valley,' said Granny Green as she got ready to leave the hotel where she had spent the last three nights with the O'Briens.

'Of course it will work,' said Mrs O'Brien.

'And you won't forget that you said we could try to fly as well,' said the twins.

'Now hold on just a second,' said Mrs O'Brien. 'I'm not sure that it's a very good idea for people of your age to be able to fly. It's different for sensible elderly people! '

'Maybe that's what Granny Green meant when she said it might not work for everyone,' sighed Maura.

'We will just have to wait and see,' said Granny Green. 'Now where can Spit have got to?'

'Miaow!' said Spit.

Granny Green and the O'Briens looked up. There, high above the entrance to the hotel, was the black cat, turning and miaowing and spitting with delight.

'Oh you clever cat!' Granny Green

cried. 'You can fly all by yourself!'

'Of course I can,' said Spit.

'And talk! He really can talk! We thought that we imagined it the other day!' laughed the twins. 'If Spit can learn both those things, we can surely learn to fly. We'd be very careful.'

'Well, we'll see,' said their parents.

'Yes, we'll see,' agreed Granny Green. Then she took a few steps backwards, ran a few steps forward and off she went, up in the air.

'Bye!' yelled the O'Briens.

'Bye!' Granny and Spit replied.

8

Another Mystery

Granny and Spit flew off across the town of Dara, back to Tigín and the entrance to the Valley of the Crows. As they gazed down on the countryside and at the people who waved and cheered, Granny Green said to Spit, 'How long exactly have you been able to talk?'

'When you say "talk", I assume that you mean "human-talk",' replied Spit. 'The ability to speak "human" came to me quite unexpectedly when you took me flying. There was just something so great about being up in the air that there seemed to be nothing that I couldn't do.'

'Like the way Mrs Fitzgerald's sight seemed to get better,' mused Granny Green. 'And I think that Miss Lynch's arthritis has got less painful, to judge from the way she has been rushing around these last few days.

'Perhaps you are right, Spit. Maybe being able to fly does mean that we can solve our health problems and develop new skills.'

'Of course it does. Check around. Ask your friends how they feel,' advised Spit. 'Maybe like me, when I knew that I could speak "human", they are too shy to say anything about it.'

'You, shy?' laughed Granny Green. 'I don't believe it!'

'Well I *am* shy, in a cat sort of way,' said Spit. 'I've known how to fly by myself for days now, only I thought that if I were to let people find out that I could fly as *well* as talk "human", they might think I was showing off. Mr Grogan, especially, might think that I was trying to get all the attention for myself.'

'Well, it was very considerate of you not to say anything until our big day was over,' said Granny Green. 'I do think it went very well, don't you?'

'Yes,' said Spit. 'But I was a little bit worried about the crows.'

'Crows?' said Granny, doing a slight sideways flip, the better to see Spit's face. 'What do you mean? I didn't see any crows anywhere.'

'Exactly,' said Spit. 'And you would have expected to see lots of them in a place called the Valley of the Crows. Unless of course it wasn't called that because of the number of crows that live there.'

'Of course it must have been named because of the number of crows,' said Granny Green. 'But you are quite right. I haven't seen or heard a bird of any kind since we started practising flying in the valley.'

'I just hope we haven't frightened them away,' said Spit. 'That could get us into mucho trouble with the bird watchers.'

' "Mucho"?' asked Granny Green. 'Where did you learn a word like that?'

'From the twins!' said Spit. 'I think they got it from a book they'd been reading about Mexico. All last winter they talked about "mucho" this and "mucho" that. Do you not remember?'

'Yes, but only very faintly,' said Granny. 'Young people nowadays seem to discover and then drop new words so quickly. But what you've said about the birds leaving the valley has me very worried. What should we do?'

'Make enquiries,' said Spit. He looked around and saw a flock of swifts swooping through the sky, chasing flies and midges. 'Let's ask this lot.'

He flew closer to the swifts and said, 'Excuse me…'

The swifts all gave a shriek of terror and dived for the safety of the dwellings where their nests were.

'Not a good move,' Spit said to Granny. 'They are not, as yet, ready for flying cats '

'Or humans either, if what you say is true,' replied Granny. 'Maybe we should approach birds at ground level.'

'Maybe we need the twins for that,' said Spit. 'They don't know how to fly so the birds might be less afraid of them. First thing in the morning, I'll nip into Dara and fetch them out to the valley … will we explain the problem to their parents?'

'Well, yes, of course. You don't think that they will object to the twins talking to the birds, do you?'

'I just wondered if they might not think it a bit odd,' said Spit. 'Did you not notice how they reacted when the twins said that they wanted to learn to fly?'

'They didn't seem to be very much in favour of it,' agreed Granny.

'They were mucho against it,' declared Spit. 'They weren't exactly happy either when they saw that I could fly *and* talk.'

'Well, it does take a bit of getting used to,' said Granny Green. 'Flying cats, flying grannies and now missing birds. No wonder they are confused.'

'Not confused,' said Spit. 'Mucho worried. What I suggest is that at first light I nip back to the hotel, have a quick chat with the twins and get them out here early before the birds are on the move. That way, we need say nothing to their parents. What do you think?'

'Mucho good,' said Granny Green. 'Very mucho good.'

9

Return of the Crows

The next morning Spit tapped first at Maura's window, then at Sean's. 'Come downstairs,' he said. 'Quickly. But no noise!'

That was easier said than done, since there were several locks and chains on the back door of the hotel that had to be opened before the twins, their eyes heavy with sleep, came out into the yard.

'What's wrong?' Maura asked in an anxious, hushed voice. 'Has Granny had an accident?'

'A flying accident? No, no, of course not,' replied Spit. 'We need help with quite a different matter. Get dressed and cycle out to Tigín as fast as you can. Leave a note for your parents - the kind

of note that won't make them worry.'

'We could say we woke early, which is true,' said Sean. 'And have gone to look for mushrooms. If we did look for mushrooms, that would be true too.'

'Too true it would,' agreed Spit. 'Now be mucho quicko or it'll be too late!'

The twins crept back upstairs, got dressed, scribbled a note, sneaked back down into the yard, closed the back door and were speeding through the empty streets and out into the country-side in less than five minutes.

Spit flew along over their heads, urging them to go faster and faster until Sean gasped, 'This is worse than being in the Tour de France bicycle race!'

'I agree,' panted Maura. 'But it must be very important for Granny Green to send for us so early in the day.'

When they heard about the missing birds in the valley, the twins knew that Granny Green and Spit had been quite right to be so worried. Granny Green and Co, not to mention Spit, would be blamed. It could be used as a reason – or an excuse – to stop them flying.

'Not everyone is overjoyed at the idea of flying grannies,' said Granny Green. 'There have been one or two rather nasty letters to the newspapers on the subject. If they discovered that *Spit* flies, there could be real trouble.'

The twins nodded in agreement. 'The only thing is, how can we talk to the birds?' asked Sean. 'If they don't speak "human", how would we understand "bird"?'

'Maybe we could learn "bird" in the same way as Spit learned to talk "human",' said Maura. 'Maybe we need to be able to fly!'

'But your parents are utterly against me teaching you how to fly,' said Granny Green. 'If I went against their wishes on this matter, they might get so upset that they wouldn't allow you even to come and visit me again.'

'Maybe we could manage to fly by ourselves,' said Sean, guessing what was in Maura's mind. 'After all, we did spend a long time watching you and the others practise. Why don't you close your eyes and count to ten?'

Granny Green and Spit closed their

eyes and counted to ten. When they opened them again, the twins had gone. So too had the big old book from the attic, which Granny Green had left on a side-table.

'Don't worry,' Spit said. 'I think that Sean and Maura know what they are doing.'

And what the twins were doing at that precise moment was cycling along the valley until they came to the old Durcan farmhouse. They leaned their bicycles against a tree and opened the book at the chapter called 'How to Fly'.

The writing was so large that it took only a few minutes to read.

When they had finished, Sean looked at Maura. And Maura looked at Sean. 'It sounds so easy,' Maura said. 'Let's try.'

Sean went first but he fell down, giving his knee a nasty scrape.

Then Maura had a go. She managed

to get off the ground but her steering was all wonky and she crashed into a blackcurrant bush.

'There must be something that we aren't doing correctly,' Sean said.

A great chorus of mocking laughter came from the surrounding trees.

Maura picked herself up. 'Who's there?' she demanded. The laughter at once stopped.

'I think it must be the crows,' said Sean.

'If it is, I don't think very much of them,' said Maura, picking leaves and berries out of her hair. 'They laugh when people get hurt but they are afraid to show their faces!'

'Beaks might be a better word than faces!' said Sean.

There was a rustle in the under-growth. A snout appeared. Then a badger's head.

'Crows are always a bit flighty,' he said. 'Easily amused, easily scared. They all flew off when the big humans started flying in the air. They told all the other birds in the valley that they were in danger of being caught and killed. Or, worse, eaten by that black cat.'

'What a load of old cabbage stalks,' said Sean, dabbing at his cut knee with a dock leaf. 'Granny Green and her friends wouldn't ever hurt anyone or anything. As for Spit, he only eats the stew that

Granny makes for him. And that has no wild birds of any kind in it.'

'So the crows have nothing to worry about?' asked the badger.

'Exactly,' said Maura. 'Are you able to tell them that?'

'Of course I am,' said the badger, and began to do a dance full of twists and grunts.

When he had finished, there was a great loud cackle from the tops of the trees. A huge cloud of crows rose into the air, blocking out the light of the sun, before taking off across the valley.

'They've got the message all right,' said the badger. 'They'll tell the other birds it's safe to come back.'

'They understood what you wanted to tell them from watching you dance?' asked Sean.

'But of course,' yawned the badger. 'Humans call it ballet. Badgers call it "rockaround".'

'But how is it that you can speak "human"?' asked Maura.

'When you've been chased and hunted by man and his hounds as many times as I have, you soon pick up the language. You have to, in order to survive,' the badger explained.

'That's terrible,' said Sean.

'I know,' said the badger.

'I thought for a second that maybe you had learned "human" in the same way as Spit did, by learning to fly,' said Maura.

'No, but I would certainly like to try my paw at it,' said the badger. 'HOW TO DO IT is all written down in this book, isn't it?'

'Yes,' said Sean, 'but I think Granny might be right when she says that flying is something only elderly people can do – or need to do.'

'It must include animals as well,' said the badger. 'After all, that cat can fly and I don't see that *he* has any special need.'

'The fact that he can fly means he can help Granny Green,' said Sean. 'He was able to fly into Dara this morning without anyone noticing. Granny Green might have wakened people.'

'Talking of which, we must think of getting back,' said Maura.

'Yes, indeed,' said Sean.

They jumped up on their bicycles.

'Just a second,' the badger called out. 'What about my flying lessons?'

The twins pretended not to hear as they cycled back to Granny Green's house. She was delighted to learn that the birds would be coming back to the Valley of the Crows.

'As regards the badger wanting to fly, she said, 'I will have to think very carefully about that, just as I will need to think carefully about the two of you trying to fly. But now, while you were in the valley, I found dozens of lovely mushrooms in the field behind the house. Spit helped me to collect them.'

'Horrid things, mushrooms,' Spit said, sniffing at his paw. 'Smelly!'

But no one at the hotel thought the beautiful fresh mushrooms were horrid.

Far from it, in fact. As the delicious aroma of fried bacon and mushrooms began to drift out from the kitchen, the hotel guests hurried down to breakfast and declared that they could think of no better way of starting the day.

'Thank heavens none of them heard Spit calling us,' said Sean.

'And thank heavens none of them knows that the badger in the Valley of the Crows wants to take flying lessons,' replied Maura.

And suddenly they both had a fit of the giggles that lasted until lunch-time.

TONY HICKEY'S BOOKS FOR THE CHILDREN'S PRESS: